Thorn in the Flesh

A Drama About a Therapy Session Gone . . . Right?

by Lowery Christopher Collins

Thorn in the Flesh

A Drama About a Therapy Session Gone . . . Right?

by Lowery Christopher Collins

Ponderlake
Publishing

THORN IN THE FLESH,
A DRAMA ABOUT A THERAPY SESSION GONE . . . RIGHT?

Written by Lowery Christopher Collins

Ponderlake Publishing: www.ponderlake.com

Playwright and/or Royalty Information: www.ChristopherCollinsOnline.com

ISBN 978-0-9992241-7-5

Thorn in the Flesh

List of Characters

MALES:
SAM, 50's, leader of the group
EUGENE, 30's, OCD
ALLEN, 30's, smoker
BILLY, late 20's, aggressive, a fighter
SHAWN, 28, addicted to human touch
TROY, 35, a body builder
MICHAEL, 47, mayor of nearby town, a pyromaniac
MATTHEW, 39, a hoarder
ANDY, 40's, a people pleaser
PAUL, 31, an adrenaline junkie
LOUIS, 37, overly obsessive, almost manic
DAVE, 32, a respected journalist
EDWIN MARTIN, 66, a judge
DARREN, 20, Edwin's son

FEMALES:
OLA, 19, SAM's daughter, mute
MABEL, 44, a chocoholic
PHYLLIS, 54, suffers from trichotillomania
HOLLY, 29, clingy and self-centered
DEANNA, 50's, in a night gown

Thorn in the Flesh

As the play begins, SAM, 50ish, and his daughter, OLA, 19, bring in food and prepare for some sort of meeting. They seem to be in good spirits.

SAM. Was there any more raisin bread in the cupboard?

OLA nods.

SAM. Good. Raisin bread works wonders. It has a calming effect. Some people eat it, and you can see their spirits settle down. Maybe we should set up raisin bread IV's for everyone in the room.

OLA laughs—large and silently.

SAM. Oh, think your old man is funny tonight, don't you? (*He is clearly pleased with his own humor.*)

OLA makes an indeterminable motion in the air with her right hand. From now own, every time she communicates, she makes the exact Same. "OLA sign" and SAM always seems to understand exactly what she means.

SAM. Really? Well, thank you very much, Sweetheart.

They continue to work.

SAM. I hope the coffee's ready. I'll go check.

OLA makes her sign.

SAM. Oh, you will? Thanks. (*He straightens while she walks out.*)

EUGENE enters SL. He is a "particular" young man, dressed neatly, articulate, mannerly.

EUGENE. Good evening, Sam.

SAM. (*Noticing him*) Hello, Eugene. Welcome. Welcome.

SAM walks over and shakes hands with EUGENE. While EUGENE willingly shakes his hand, it is obvious that it makes him slightly uncomfortable to do so.

SAM. Good job, Eugene. Very good job. I could hardly notice.

EUGENE. Thank you. (*Smiles*)

SAM. (*Getting back to work.*) If you'll excuse me, I have to get everything ready for tonight.

EUGENE. Of course. I know. I do know. I'm here early, as usual. Can't stand to be late. Well, can't stand to be on time. Have to be here early, early, early. Check things out, see where things are and where . . . they should be.

SAM. I know, Eugene. You're fine. I'm sure people will be arriving any minute.

EUGENE. (*Begins straightening the chairs that are already in a half circle—getting each one JUST right*) Oh, I doubt that will be any minute. I'm usually unusually early, terribly early. Quite the opposite of being tardy. I don't even like that word: tardy. Sounds like a death sentence.

SAM. (*Working*) Now, Eugene, doesn't that sound a little extreme?

EUGENE. You're right, Sam. That's too much again. It's just not desirable or acceptable for me.

SAM. Well put.

OLA enters with raisin bread.

She waves at EUGENE.

EUGENE. Good evening, Ola. How nice to see you!

OLA signs.

SAM. She returns the sentiment.

EUGENE. Thank you, Ola. Is that raisin bread? Raisin bread has just a nice flavor. For some reason, I feel better after a slice. I can't really explain it. It makes me feel, well, better.

SAM. I agree, Eugene. You are more than welcome to some. Would you like a slice now?

EUGENE. Oh, no. It's not appropriate. We're not officially here yet. Nothing has started.

SAM. Eugene, it doesn't really matter. We . . .

EUGENE. No, that's for everyone and for when everyone arrives. For me to . . .

SAM. Okay, Eugene.

EUGENE. I just think there is a certain order to the way things are to be done, that manners dictate that we are to behave a certain way.

SAM. That's fine, Eugene. You *are* a gentleman.

OLA signs.

SAM. And Ola agrees.

EUGENE. Thank you, both. That means quite a lot coming from the two of you. I strive so hard to . . . Sam?

SAM. Yes?

EUGENE. May I help you organize this table? This row of bread has twelve slices, but this one has ten. I know there are different sizes, but in each case if we could just make sure that . . . well, you know.

SAM. That's fine. Organize all you want.

EUGENE. Oh, Sam. (*Working*) Thank you. That makes me feel so much better. I can't stand for things to be . . . I mean . . . for things to appear to be . . . or . . .

SAM. No need for explanations. I understand.

From SL, ALLEN enters, mid-30's dressed casually.

ALLEN. Yo, guys. How's it going?

SAM. Hi, Allen. How are you tonight?

ALLEN. Pretty good, Sam. Hi, Ola.

She waves.

15

ALLEN. Hi, Eugene.

EUGENE. (*Friendly, but preoccupied with straightening*) Oh, hi, Allen. You're early.

SAM. Yeah, you are. Eugene is the only one to get here this early.

ALLEN. Yeah, had an early dinner with the missus 'cause she has some kind of women's meeting to go to, quilts, sewing, some stuff where she meets with some old ladies at a sewing shop. I don't know. A girl's club. (*His mind is on EUGENE, working frantically.*) Um, Eugene, what 'cha up to over there?

EUGENE. Huh? Oh, just organizing. Making sure the rows of cookies and crackers look fine.

ALLEN. Oh, okay. Sam. (*talking lower*)

SAM. Yes?

ALLEN. (*Even lower*) Think he should be doing that?

SAM. What do you mean?

ALLEN. You know. With his problem and all. Isn't that kinda playing right in the hands of what he needs to fix.

SAM. Don't worry. It's minor. Plus, it may be a good exercise in coping, dealing with things on a small level.

ALLEN. You're the boss.

SAM. Not the boss, Allen.

ALLEN. You know what I mean.

SAM. We're not here to bring trouble. This is laid back. We're just here to help each other.

EUGENE. Look at this, Sam. Now how does that look?

SAM. (*Looking*) Like a masterpiece, Eugene. Balance and beauty. You could be a caterer, Eugene.

EUGENE. You really think so?

SAM. I do.

EUGENE. I never thought about that before. Allen, look at the spread.

ALLEN. Looks good, Eugene. Classy.

EUGENE. Classy. Nice.

ALLEN. Just don't get your feelings hurt when it doesn't look that nice after LOUIS gets through with it.

EUGENE. (*to SAM.*) Is *he* coming tonight?

SAM. Louis?

EUGENE. Yes, Battleship Louis. Is he coming?

SAM. As far as I know, yes.

EUGENE breathes loudly and with frustration.

SAM. Everyone has a place here, Eugene. I know he irritates you.

EUGENE looks at SAM. as if to say, "Are you serious??? Why are you understating the issue so badly????"

SAM. I know. But things are better.

ALLEN. He hasn't said anything to you in the past several meetings. I know he's rude, but we've got you covered.

SAM. I think we've managed to have a balance of freedom and openness without cruelty and judgment. That's what we're here for.

EUGENE. I know. He's just so . . .

SAM. I know. We all know.

OLA signs.

SAM. OLA says she knows, too.

MABEL enters from SL. She is dressed nicely. It's obvious that she is a paraprofessional from the business world, still in her office attire. She is intelligent, but a little mousy.

MABEL. Salutations, dear friends.

SAM. Welcome, Mabel.

EUGENE. Oh, Mabel. It's good to see you.

ALLEN. Hi, Mabel.

OLA waves.

SAM. How are you tonight? *(He goes to help her with her coat and purse.)* May I take these for you?

MABEL. A gentleman as always. Thank you, Sam. Thank you.

SAM. No problem.

EUGENE goes up to her and gives her an air hug. She reciprocates.

EUGENE. Did you make it through the week?

MABEL. It was tough, but I did.

EUGENE. Did you get my email?

MABEL. I did. Thank you.

EUGENE. Well, I figured you needed some encouragement. When I found out, I thought, "Oh, Mabel." I hated to bring it up, but I figured: you're a grown woman. You can handle it. I just wanted to show my support.

ALLEN. What happened?

EUGENE. I'm sorry I brought it up.

MABEL. It's okay. I survived it.

EUGENE. I'm so proud of you.

ALLEN. Is it a secret?

MABEL. No, it's just that last Thursday was National . . . Chocolate Cake Day.

ALLEN. Oh.

MABEL. And all around the office, people were bringing in everything you can imagine. Those people don't miss a celebration. If it's jellybean day, you'll slip and fall on those little buggers. If it's World Kite Day, you can bet your bottom dollar there will be box kites, traditional kites, square kites, round kites, Chinese kites, dog kites, cat kites everywhere you look. I swear: on Cinco de Mayo, the entire office smelled like cilantro and looked like a piñata had exploded everywhere. I don't know how these people have time to work. Every day, there's something to celebrate. But Thursday was hard. The smell was everywhere. It was, it was . . .

EUGENE. It'll be okay, Mabel. You survived.

MABEL. Yes, I burned incense. I used cotton balls in my nose. I did what I had to do. But I didn't succumb.

SAM. Good for you, Mabel. You're strong.

MABEL. Thank you, Sam.

SAM. That's the kind of determination we talk about here every week. You're living it.

ALLEN. Good for you, Mabel.

MABEL. I'm not going to lie. It wasn't easy.

SHAWN and MATTHEW enter the meeting room from SL at the same time. SHAWN, 27, is an affable man, looks normal by most accounts, but has an addiction to human touch. As he interacts, it is obvious that he still fights a need to touch everyone he finds himself near. MATTHEW, 30, dressed a little down, while friendly, appears to struggle interacting with most people. It's evident that these two have become friends.

SHAWN. Yeah, I know. I've wondered the same thing all my life. I mean how do the cones stay on.

MATTHEW. Exactly, I mean, exactly.

ALLEN. Hi, guys.

SAM. Hello, gentlemen.

SHAWN and MATTHEW greet the group: "Hey, everybody, Hi," etc.

EUGENE. Hello

MABEL. Hi, guys.

OLA waves.

ALLEN. Ready for another session?

MATTHEW. (*without enthusiasm*) Thrilled.

SHAWN. Ah, come on. (*hits him on the arm*)

MATTHEW. Ow.

SHAWN. Cry baby.

MATTHEW. Am not.

SHAWN. I'm not going down that road.

SAM. We have a new group member. You can't be hitting people like that in front of him.

SHAWN. Are you kidding me?

EUGENE. Someone new? No.

SAM. Eugene, we've talked about this.

EUGENE. I know.

SAM. We're in for a few changes tonight.

EUGENE. More??

MABEL. Sounds like a deviation from our usual roller-coaster ride.

SAM. We'll be fine. I think it'll be productive.

EUGENE. (*with skepticism*) Productive.

SAM. EUGENE.

EUGENE. (*with reluctant acceptance*) Productive.

SAM. SHAWN, can you help me with the table for a minute?

EUGENE. The table's finished, Sam. Everything's exact. (*panicking*)

SAM. It's okay, Eugene. We won't bother anything you've done. I know it's all set up.

EUGENE. It's perfect.

SAM. I know. We won't touch your artwork.

SHAWN walks with SAM. over to the table. EUGENE stares at them for a few seconds to make sure that they don't disturb the work he had done earlier. He then begins to straighten all the chairs in the room, arranging them in an exact semi-circle. MABEL sits in one of the chairs, pulls out a small notebook, and begins to write. As EUGENE straightens, the fact that MABEL is sitting in the middle of his work zone clearly disturbs him. Yet, he is careful not to voice his concerns. ALLEN stands near MATTHEW, who is clearly uncomfortable with the fact that SHAWN has moved to the other side of the room. ALLEN takes out a package of gum.

ALLEN. Want one?

MATTHEW. Huh?

ALLEN. Gum? Want a piece?

MATTHEW. Oh, no. Thank you. I'm gonna wait for the buffet.

ALLEN. Gotcha. (*He puts a piece in his mouth.*) I'm gonna go ahead and indulge in both. I'll tell you: I chew so much of this gum I keep the whole industry in business.

MATTHEW. (*trying to pay attention*) Well, if that's what it takes to cope, it's better than the alternative.

SAM. How's he doing?

SHAWN. Better I think. It's hard to get him talking about much of substance. I can manage to get him to the meetings, but that's all.

ALLEN looks for a place to throw the wrapper away. This action demands MATTHEW's full attention now.

MATTHEW. Oh, would you like for me to take that for you?

ALLEN. I'm just seeing if there's some place to toss this.

MATTHEW. I can take it for you.

ALLEN. There's really no need for you to take it. It's just trash that I have to find a . . . (*realizes that MATTHEW, as a hoarder, is wanting to collect trash*) Oh, Matthew. You know I can't give you this.

MATTHEW. (*irritated*). Okay, okay.

ALLEN. You can't have things like this just to . . .

MATTHEW. (*loud whisper*) Shhh. Okay, okay, okay. Alright already. I know. I know. I know. I don't broadcast that you're wanting to smoke again.

ALLEN. Whoa. I haven't said a word about wanting to smoke.

MATTHEW. You chewed gum.

ALLEN. I chewed *gum*.

MATTHEW. You chewed gum because you want to smoke.

ALLEN. I chew gum because I . . .

MATTHEW. . . . are dealing with not smoking.

ALLEN. I'm chewing gum.

MATTHEW. Exactly.

ALLEN. And you want this piece of trash gum wrapper to take home with you to add to your collection of trash you've hoarded for ten years.

MATTHEW. Do you see a gum wrapper in my hand?

ALLEN. Only because I refused to give it to you.

SAM. Gentlemen, gentlemen, let's calm down.

ALLEN. Sam, I'm not going to put up with this.

MATTHEW. I'm standing here minding my own business and once again to have to deal with criticism. I can just go home.

ALLEN. *I* can just go home.

SAM. No one needs to go home.

MATTHEW. I'm standing here empty-handed. I have nothing in my hands. I have nothing that I'm trying to take home.

SAM. It's okay, Matthew. No one is accusing you of anything. Just calm down.

MATTHEW. And he's chewing gum.

ALLEN. I can chew gum. There's nothing anywhere that says I can't chew gum.

SAM. You're perfectly okay. Don't worry about it. We are not here to police anyone. We're just here to talk and to help each other.

MATTHEW. I'm just saying. I don't have anything. I'm standing here empty-handed.

ALLEN. And I'm just chewing the stick of gum. And I still have the wrapper.

SAM. Okay. Let's just take a time out. Allen, would you mind going to see if Ola needs any help in the kitchen?

ALLEN. Sure thing.

ALLEN goes to the kitchen.

SAM. Let's just find some place to settle down.

EUGENE sits near MABEL and glances at her notebook in which she continues to write. She notices and shows her consternation.

BILLY and PAUL enter SL. BILLY is addicted to fighting, and his very demeanor shows that fact. PAUL is addicted to taking risks, adrenaline. Likewise, his personal issues show with every action and word.

BILLY. What you're planning on doing you cannot do.

PAUL. Oh, I can.

EUGENE. You can't say that.

BILLY. What?

EUGENE. You can't say that statement that way.

PAUL. We're having a conversation about . . .

EUGENE. I don't care about the content of your conversation.

PAUL. What?

EUGENE. I don't care about the content of your conversation. I was referring to how you said what you said.

PAUL. Are you crazy?

EUGENE. It depends upon whom you ask. The statement you made: "What you're planning on doing you cannot do" is syntactically and grammatically incorrect. It should have been phrased "You cannot do what you're planning on doing." The basic sentence construction was weak and inherently flawed. A simple switching of the clauses repairs the construction and salvages the sentiment.

BILLY. Who are you?

EUGENE. Eugene Densworth Robertson

BILLY. Well, Eugene Densworth Robertson, shut your trap.

SAM. So, are you Billy?

BILLY. Yeah, I am. Who are you?

SAM. I'm Sam Kessler. I lead the sessions around here.

BILLY. Oh. Nice to meet you, I guess. Billy Pender here.

SAM. No need for last names here. We strive for anonymity.

BILLY. But you've heard of me?

SAM. It's just that Judge Martin told me you were coming tonight. (*to PAUL*) And Dr. Lacey told me to expect a young man named Paul.

PAUL. That's me. (*extends his hand to SAM.*).

SAM. I do ask that you refrain from using profanity or from arguing or insulting each other.

BILLY. I can keep from ripping someone's head off if he can keep from talking to me when I don't want him to.

PAUL. We'll be good, Sammy. We just need a little respect.

SAM. Sam. Sam is fine. And this place is all about respect.

PAUL. Well, we'll do fine. We'll do fine.

SHAWN. We're in for a fun evening.

MATTHEW. Evidently.

BILLY. What's that supposed to mean?

SAM. Every meeting that we have is filled with personality and life. That's one of our goals.

ALLEN. *(re-entering from the kitchen with OLA)* When is this hothead supposed to be getting here?

MABEL. *(trying to cover for him)* You mean that new doctor with the temper problems?

ALLEN. No, I mean the new patient with the . . .

MABEL. You're so funny, Allen. You know that it's a doctor that we were talking about.

ALLEN. I could have sworn that . . .

MABEL. No. Doctor. End of discussion.

MATTHEW. What is this?

SHAWN. Health insurance.

BILLY. You got some snotty doctor showing up tonight gonna cause some problems?

SAM. *(Looks at Mable, knowing she made everything up—to keep the peace)* I guess it's possible . . . now.

BILLY. If you need me to take care of things if he gets out of hand, just let me know. I can bust a few heads. I don't care if he is a doc.

SAM. Well, we're not hoping for violence in any way.

BILLY. I'm just yanking your chain, Sam. I know why I'm here.

MICHAEL, wearing a suit, overcoat, hat, and sunglasses enters.

SAM. Michael.

MICHAEL. Sam.

SAM. Can I take your hat and coat?

MICHAEL. Not yet. I have to see who's out front.

SAM. I don't think anybody's out there. We've been here week after week, and no one is ever out there.

MICHAEL. Every week holds new surprises.

SAM. MICHAEL, if anything, we're confidential here.

MICHAEL. I trust you, Sam. There are just a lot of people in this group, a lot of people. Speaking of which, I think three more are headed in. (*walking away*) Why in the world did I get stuck in this?

MABEL. I ask myself that question every time I come here.

SHAWN. That's the truth.

ALLEN. Yep.

PAUL. What have we gotten ourselves into?

Enter a group of people stage left. In the group is TROY, who is obviously addicted to bodybuilding, ANDY, who is addicted to people pleasing, and PHYLLIS, who has trichotillomania.
TROY is in his mid-20s. ANDY is in his mid-40s. And PHYLLIS is 63.

SAM. Hello, everyone. How are you tonight?

ANDY. (*Stuttering a bit*) Doing fine, Sam. Doing fine.

PHYLLIS. Oh, Sam. Just fine tonight. So nice to see you.

SAM. And you as well, Phyllis.

PHYLLIS. Oh, Ola. How are you dear? How are you dear?

OLA makes her normal sign. SAM watches her and then interprets.

SAM. She says that she's having a nice night.

OLA makes the same exact sign again.

SAM. She also says that she has had a cold but she's feeling a lot better.

PHYLLIS. Ola, I'm so glad to see you're feeling better then. (*She walks over to OLA and hugs her.*)

SAM. And you, Troy?

TROY. Pardon?

SAM. Are you okay tonight?

TROY. Oh, yes, sir. I'm good.

MICHAEL. (*approaching SAM.*) May I have a word with you in private?

SAM. Well, we're about to get started.

MICHAEL. It's important, and it'll only take a few seconds.

SAM. Okay. Guys, go ahead and get a snack if you want to and then take a seat. We need
to get started.

SAM. and MICHAEL walk down left, away from the crowd.

SAM. What's up, Michael?

MICHAEL. I don't mean to be paranoid about all of this every single meeting, but I'm a
little concerned.

SAM. About?

MICHAEL. You know I have a reputation to uphold. I trust you. You've proven to me
that I can trust you. It took me a long time to get used to these other people being
in this meeting. However, I know that's what I'm forced to do based upon my
situation. And I think that I have willingly and gracefully accepted that reality.
But yet another reality is my position and my personal situation. You know what
I'm talking about.

SAM. We've had this conversation, Micahel. You know that I have respected you and the
delicacy of your situation. What exactly are you talking about this time?

MICHAEL. Two extra people. Those two guys over there. Are they new? Who are they?
I just need to know.

SAM. Those are two new members of our group. They are supposed to be here.
Everything is legal and on the up and up.

MICHAEL. This group just keeps getting larger and larger. When everything started, I
was under the impression that this would be a one-on-one situation. However, it's
growing into something much different.

SAM. Michael, you know I have nothing to do with the fact that you were assigned to
this group. You know what this group is. You know the implications for its
success. You were just lucky enough to be chosen for this situation. We are doing
everything in our power, I am doing everything in my power, to make this work
and to protect you and everyone here.

MICHAEL. (*calming down*) Those are just two new patients then?

SAM. Group members.

MICHAEL. Group members.

SAM. Yes. That's all. Group members.

MICHAEL. (*Calm*) okay. I'm sorry to get so upset, Sam. You know the situation. I'm just a little worried still.

SAM. I understand completely, Michael. I know your situation. You're doing perfectly fine. Let's get back to things. (*Now turning his attention and remarks to the entire group*) All right, everybody. Are we ready to get started?

EUGENE. Where's Louis?

SAM. Has anyone heard from Louis?

No one responds.

SAM. Evidently not. I hope he's okay.

MABEL. I'm sure he's fine. He's a tough one.

ALLEN. Louis?

SHAWN. I wouldn't use the word "tough."

MABEL. You know what I mean.

MICHAEL. Can we get started?

SAM. Everybody, take a seat please.

People move to the seats. BILLY and PAUL take seats across the semicircle from SAM., evidently sitting in SHAWN's and MATTHEW's seats. SHAWN and MATTHEW are obviously upset that they have to find somewhere new to sit.

SAM. So, how is everyone doing tonight?

Several people answer: "fine, good, okay, fair," etc.

SAM. Good to hear. It's good to see that everyone made it here safely tonight.

EUGENE. Not everyone.

SAM. It's not a prison, Eugene. We're here to talk. There's probably a good explanation as to why Louis isn't here. Until then, we move on. Ola, no phone calls?

OLA signs.

SAM. Really? Who answered the phone?

OLA signs.

SAM. Good. We're just using this facility. We shouldn't be dealing with much, just a call if someone can't make it.

OLA signs.

SAM. Right. Good girl.

BILLY. Wait a minute. What did she just . . .?

PAUL. Was that some sort of . . . ?

PHYLLIS. Everyone has her own gifts.

BILLY. Gifts?

ANDY. It's so nice that we can get along with each other in such harmony.

PAUL. But she just . . .

MABEL. Had a conversation with her dad.

ALLEN. Very well, I might add.

MICHAEL. As she always does.

TROY. Every meeting night.

PAUL. But she . . .

MATTHEW. It's no use. Don't fight it.

BILLY. Did you say "fight"?

SAM. There's no fight.

EUGENE. I want to go home.

MATTHEW. Home is more fun.

SHAWN. But not as productive.

MICHAEL. Wanna bet?

SAM. Michael?

PAUL. Michael? You look familiar.

MICHAEL. (*in frustration, to Sam*) See??

SAM. It's okay. We're about anonymity here.

EUGENE. We'll see how far that goes.

PHYLLIS. Have you ever had anything shared outside of this group?

EUGENE. Not that I know of.

SAM. Okay, okay. Let's get back to our focus for tonight.

MICHAEL. Is it possible at this point?

SAM. We have a lot to cover.   As you all know by now, we have two new members of our group tonight.

MICHAEL. The more the merrier.

SAM. Michael, we've discussed this.

MICHAEL. I know.

SAM. It's about trust.

SHAWN, MATTHEW, EUGENE, ALLEN, TROY, ANDY, and PHYLLIS. Trust.
(*They all look at each other, surprised they all said that at the same time.*)

SAM. Well, as I said: we have two new members here tonight who I'm sure are wondering what they've gotten themselves into.

MATTHEW. Just two?

SAM. Billy is here tonight to join our ranks.

BILLY. Not by choice.

MICHAEL. Tell me about it.

SAM. He's dealing with some issues that Judge Martin thought could be helped by our little group.

ALLEN. It's not that little any more.

ANDY. But it's comfortable. So comfortable.

MATTHEW. I wouldn't go that far.

SHAWN. Let's cut to the chase then. (*to BILLY*) What's your issue?

BILLY. Issue?

SHAWN. Flaw? Problem? Addiction?

BILLY. Guess.

SHAWN. Pardon?

BILLY. Guess what my "flaw" is.

EUGENE. Just one?

BILLY. You're about to face a world of hurt.

EUGENE. But you can't, can you?

BILLY. What??

EUGENE. That's the very thing you're here for, isn't it? To deal with your anger. To learn not to fight.

BILLY. (*Stops*) That's why they sent me. (*Beat.*) But I still do what I want. If I see a need, I deal with it.

SAM. But not here. Billy, this is a place to stop and think. Eugene, this is a place for you not to provoke.

EUGENE. As usual.

SAM. As always.

BILLY. I didn't drive here for somebody is sit there and talk down to me. I don't take to that too well.

PAUL. (*to MICHAEL*) You're the mayor of Manchester!

MICHAEL. Good grief! (*Head in hands*)

PAUL. I saw you at the ribbon cutting of that pizzeria on Parker.

MICHAEL. Sam!

SAM. It's okay, Michael. Almost everyone here has known that you're the mayor of a nearby town.

PAUL. Manchester.

SAM. Yes, but no, we don't want to name names.

PAUL. You're a pretty important dude. Weren't you on that committee to re-elect the governor?

MICHAEL. (*hyperventilating*) Dear, Lord.

SHAWN. You were on the committee to re-elect the governor?

ANDY. That's great, Michael.

MABEL. I voted on the other guy.

MATTHEW. Me, too.

MICHAEL. I need to go home.

SAM. Please, Michael. Calm down. You'll be okay. Everyone, please. Let's not talk details about each other's personal lives. That's not what we're here to do.

EUGENE. We're not here to talk about things that are personal to us?

ALLEN. Isn't that why we're here in the first place?

SAM. You know what I mean. Identity. Issues of privacy.

MATTHEW. Like names, alliances, and committees.

SAM. Exactly.

BILLY. I hate the governor.

PHYLLIS. Oh, I really think he's a breath of fresh air.

SAM. Okay, hate's a strong word.

MABEL. More like rank air.

EUGENE. I'm more concerned with record than with personality.

ANDY. I love a good personality.

MICHAEL. Can we leave my professional relationships out of this?!

MABEL. I can't believe you like him.

TROY. Can we please get off this topic? I'm very uncomfortable.

SAM. Yes! We do NOT need to discuss anything political in this group.

BILLY. You're ruling out a lot of different topics of conversation, Sammy.

SAM. Sam. And we are not here for this. We have to move on.

TROY. Thank you.

ALLEN. We still don't know about this other dude.

EUGENE. I detest that word. You're using it because you heard Mike Tyson use it a minute ago.

ALLEN. I use "dude" all the time.

BILLY. Mike Tyson? What that directed toward me?

EUGENE. If the tattoo fits . . .

BILLY. You're really trying my patience.

SAM. BILLY.

BILLY. If I weren't in this meeting and if I didn't like Mike Tyson, I'd show you some "what for" on your "what not!"

EUGENE. My what?

BILLY. Dude!

EUGENE. (*covering his ears*) Stop!

SAM. GENTLEMEN!!!!!! This is not a free-for-all!!!!! We are here to get some things done. We're here to have a little calm, therapeutic conversation. We're here for you and your families and for the sake of your lives. I cannot and will not put up with chaos and condescension. Is that understood?

EVERYONE ELSE (*except OLA, PAUL, and BILLY*): Yes, Sam.

SAM. Now . . .

ALLEN. So, who's the dude?

EUGENE drops his head between his knees for several seconds. ALLEN grins from ear to ear.

SAM. Our other new member is Paul.

A few people say hello to PAUL, who is mildly cordial.

SAM. Just like every one of you here, Paul has been assigned to attend our meetings—I think by the same person who assigned each of you.

SHAWN. (*to PAUL*) What's your wicked story?

PAUL. Wicked. Good word. Good word. I'm just a guy.

MATTHEW. "Just a guy" dudes (*EUGENE moans*) don't get invited to little meetings like ours.

SAM. Paul has a special need that some of you may identify with.

PAUL. I would bet money nobody here identifies with what I do.

SAM. We never know.

ALLEN. Now, you've just got me curious.

SAM. PAUL has a situation in which . . .

PAUL. Just tell it like it is, Sam, my man. I am addicted to the rush, whether it's adrenaline or the thrill or what, I'm going for the biggies: hard-core par core,

34

bungie jumping, skydiving. You name it: I do it all, all the time.

TROY. That sounds . . .

MICHAEL. Dangerous

EUGENE. Stupid.

TROY. Amazing

SAM. But as extremes go, Paul finds himself here with us.

PAUL. I know it got a little out of hand. I live life on the edge a bit too much.

EUGENE. Is that why you two are friends?

SAM. Eugene, please. Again. No judgment.

PAUL. (*to EUGENE*) I see that you're here in the group, yourself for some reason. And I'm seeing why.

SAM. Okay! Ola, is something smoking in the kitchen? I smell something.

OLA goes to check.

SAM. Guys, we have an interesting and eventful night. We have to get started.

MICHAEL. I don't know if I like the sound of that.

SHAWN. We're all ears, boss-man.

ANDY. With you 100%, boss-man.

TROY. I'd really like to get started.

MABEL. I've been quiet here a long time, but I have to say, there's some real insanity in this room.

PHYLLIS. I do hope you're talking about statements that have been made.

MABEL. The whole shebang, Phyllis. The whole shebang.

SAM. We all deal with our own situations. And now we have our stories out there. We know.

PAUL. We don't know about these other people.

BILLY. And we don't want to.

MICHAEL. Exactly. I mean exactly. We don't. But we're forced to.

SAM. We're here because we have each been assigned to be here. I don't know why we have the combination that we have, but there's a reason.

EUGENE. You're convinced of that?

SAM. Yes. For some reason, I've received the court orders for this combination of people. We're here to do what we've been asked to do.

MATTHEW. That makes us sound like guinea pigs.

SAM. No.

ALLEN. Pretty much. I mean: I like to smoke. I like to smoke way too much. There was a point in time in which I went through four or five packs a day.

BILLY. Five?

ALLEN. Yeah. A few years back. But that's not my point. I'm just saying: I smoked a lot. I fought it, but to be assigned to come to one of these groups because of cigarettes?? I'm still not over that.

SAM. We've talked about this before. It got out of hand for you.

ALLEN. I'm not denying that. I've never denied that. But cigarettes, Sam. Cigarettes.

SAM. And because of what happened because of those cigarettes, right? I never assigned you to this group.

ALLEN. I know. I'm not blaming you. I just get it. And it's a court order.

SAM. It's a court order on everyone here. That's part of the point I think.

EUGENE. Why?

SAM. Look. I even was appointed to this. There are more pressing issues in my life that I'm dealing with right now, but we do what's expected of us, and I am here to help you in any way that I can: not just because I have to, but because I want to. Ola and I don't have to go to the trouble we do to feed you, but we do.

ANDY. We love it!

PHYLLIS. We're not griping at you, Sam. It's just not quite fair.

TROY. What kind of "progress" are they expecting? I mean: is it possible?

SAM. I think we talk through a lot of things.

MATTHEW. But does that do any good?

SAM. You don't think so?

ANDY. I do!

EUGENE. We know *you* do, Andy.

MABEL. I don't feel any better.

SAM. This has to be beneficial to someone.

ALLEN. It's not you, Sam. I do think it's great to talk with each other about dealing with the things we're having issues with, but I don't understand the fact that it's mandatory.

MATTHEW. Some of us would rather be sitting in our homes.

SAM. Would you really, Matthew?

SHAWN. Matthew, come on, man.

MATTHEW. I mean. I don't mind seeing you guys, but I don't like talking about . . .

MICHAEL. Things you don't talk about with strangers!

PHYLLIS. I don't think we're "strangers."

BILLY. Yeah. We are.

SHAWN. Well, you two are, but not for long.

PAUL. It's not like we have a choice.

SAM. We don't. But we can make it less unpleasant.

ANDY. I think so!

SAM. Guys, we have a few things to cover tonight, but before we introduce the other group members to Paul and Billy, there's something I need to tell you.

37

MICHAEL. (*Head in his hands*) Lord help us.

SHAWN. It might not be bad.

ANDY. Right!

MICHAEL. Is it bad?

SAM. I guess it's up for interpretation.

MICHAEL. Good grief.

SAM. It's not bad. It's just something new.

MATTHEW. New is bad.

PHYLLIS. New is not bad.

MABEL. New is always bad.

SAM. It's not bad.

OLA signs to SAM. He watches.

SAM. Yes. It's what we talked about, Ola.

BILLY. (*to PAUL*) What they talked about?

PAUL. You and the girl?

SAM. Yes. That's my daughter, Ola.

PHYLLIS. Such a wonderful old-fashioned name.

PAUL. Ola? Is she deaf.

OLA looks at him.

SAM. No. She's just . . . been mute for a while.

PAUL. You married?

EUGENE. Oh, my gosh!

SHAWN. What's with the questions?

ALLEN. Yeah.

PAUL. Can't a guy be curious? I mean, evidently you guys share everything except underwear around here. I was just wondering a few things.

PHYLLIS. But Sam is our . . .

SAM. It's okay. Ola, can you step into the kitchen for a bit?

OLA does so.

ALLEN. You don't have to explain all the . . .

SAM. It's okay. Really. Well, Paul, yes, I'm married. And my wife is very much still with us. She's at home right now. In fact, every so often, Ola steps out to go check on her. That's possible because we live just two houses down to the left. Perhaps you saw it when you came in: little house, brick, green shutters, front-entrance driveway. It's amazing we have that house, so close. It's the only reason that I'm able to do things like this tonight. It seemed to fall right into our laps. I'm a counselor, have been for a while, but my wife and my daughter are the most important things in my life. My wife is home right now in the bedroom, curtains closed, covers pulled up, medicated as best we can, suffering from an extended migraine she's had continuously for years.

PAUL. For years?

SAM. For years. Doctors can't cure her. They can't figure out why she has it. Medication barely helps, but even if it helps a little, it's worth it. There's nothing that anyone knows to do besides be there, keep things dark and cool, and try to help in any way possible.

PHYLLIS. Is there nothing that works, Sam?

SAM. Nothing. And it's just solid pain. There's nothing to be done in a hospital that she can't get at home, so I keep her as comfortable as possible. I do what I can here, since I've been court-appointed myself, for some reason known only to someone. I do this and then tend to her.

BILLY. For years?

SAM. Years. It started on a vacation several years ago. She started feeling very weak and dizzy, and the headaches began—one after another until the last ones never stopped.

EUGENE. That's just horrible.

SAM. It was near that time, I stopped hearing OLA's voice. She'd open her mouth to say something, and nothing would come out. After a while, nothing even "looked" like words, and she stopped. I'm just thankful she tries to communicate with me in her own way.

ANDY. You're a brave man.

SAM. It's not bravery. You deal. And that's what we're here to do. Deal.

MABEL. We all do. I never would have dreamed I could get addicted to chocolate. I ate it—like anyone else, but a few years back, I started these horrible cravings for it—all the time. It's all I thought about. Allen, if you wonder why YOU are here for cigarettes, imagine being here for loving chocolate.

SAM. But Mabel, it's more than love.

MABEL. I know. It's obsession that leads to bad things. I'm not so arrogant as to think I don't need to tackle it. I just don't like having to.

MATTHEW. Exactly. I like my stuff.

SHAWN. Dude, you just said that out loud.

EUGENE. ARGH! Don't say "dude."

SHAWN, BILLY, PAUL, and TROY. Dude.

EUGENE. Stop.

SHAWN. You just said you like your stuff.

MATTHEW. Of course, I do. There. I said it. Why is everything an interrogation?

MABEL. Because that's what life is.

MICHAEL. That's the truth!

ANDY. I agree!

PHYLLIS starts pulling out her hair.

SAM. Phyllis.

MABEL. Phyllis.

SAM. Let me handle this.

PHYLLIS. Oh, I'm sorry. I slipped.

SAM. It's okay. Just relax.

TROY. I still want to be bigger.

BILLY. What?

TROY. I tell myself all the time that I don't need to, but I do. I need more mass. I try, Sam. I really try. But I can't. I can't tell myself it's not important. It may not be important to anyone else, but I want to build myself up. I know I'm supposed to tell myself and to tell you and to tell the group that I don't need to, that's it's not important, but it is of utmost importance to me. See. I admit it. I need more muscle. I need more mass. I need more . . . manliness. Oh. This is not working. No offense. I like you, Sam. You're a good man.

ANDY. He is!!

TROY. Shut up. You're a good man, but I don't know if I can keep this up. I can lie to you and to Suck-Up here and to the mayor and the Chocoholic and the Fire-breathing hair eater. I can pretend for Puff Daddy and for the OCD master, but I can't lie to myself. I need more.

SAM. Well, Troy. Thank you for your honesty. I think that's the first time I've ever seen you come out and say that much. It took courage. I do think, however, that you *have* made headway. The fact that you said those things means you're thinking through the process and what it *should* look like for you as person, not just the group.

PAUL. (*to BILLY*) He's better than I thought.

SAM. *But*, before we get too deep into discussions, there's the matter of what I need to tell you.

MICHAEL. That which doesn't make us stronger kills us.

EUGENE. You have that backward.

MICHAEL. No, I don't.

SAM. As you know, each person here, myself included, is here by court order and assignment.

MATTHEW. We do know that.

MICHAEL. Indeed.

SAM. And not one of us, myself included, is aware of exactly why this specific group make up is the way it is. Unlike, drug dependency groups or AA, we represent a wide variety of . . . issues . . . that seem to have very little in common other that the fact that we each deal with things that have taken over our very psyches. I mean, you've admitted as such. You don't smoke a lot. You smoke a LOT.

ALLEN. Smoked. Past tense.

SAM. But you want to.

ALLEN. With all my heart.

SAM. And Mabel, you don't LIKE chocolate. You'd marry it if you could.

MABEL. As soon as it becomes legal in Massachusetts.

ANDY. That's where I was born!

MABEL. Figures.

SAM. In each of your cases, it's not even an obsession. It takes over each minute. You make plans how to betray and hinder any solutions to fix things--so that you can succumb to your . . . addiction, for lack of a better word.

BILLY. I'd fight anybody, anytime, all the time. Grannies, toddlers, preachers, teachers, mommas, daddies, anyone, any level—if I wouldn't go to jail for it.

MICHAEL. Wow.

MABEL. Wow.

BILLY. What?

SAM. Think about it a lot?

BILLY. Huh? Uh, yeah. All the time.

SAM. Same for the adrenaline rush?

PAUL. Yep.

SAM. For each of us who's been here, we've tried to deal with the exact thing that has come to define our quirks or addictions. Some haven't dealt with things as openly as others.

EUGENE. Matthew.

MATTHEW. What?

EUGENE. Well, you haven't.

MATTHEW. Lay off. I'm fine.

EUGENE. That's why you're here?

MATTHEW. I said "lay off."

SHAWN. Back off, Eugene.

PAUL. So, you're a hoarder?

MATTHEW. What?!

PAUL. Hoarder. Saving every little thing. Living in a house filled to the ceiling with crap? That's you, right?

MATTHEW. I live in my . . . I live in my own house. I pay for that house. I . . .

SHAWN. It's okay.

PAUL. Hoard. It's okay to admit. I mean everybody here knows. I mean, if I figured it out in fifteen minutes, these guys know it already.

MATTHEW. I live in my . . .

PAUL. Your house. I know. I'm not judging you, man. Fill that baby to the roof. I don't care. It's your life.

SAM. Okay. Yes, we ALL deal with issues that seem to be taking their toll on our daily lives. We discuss them every week. And we're the lucky ones who were assigned to each other. But I honestly think it's been working.

MICHAEL. You do?

SAM. I do.

ALLEN. (*to MICHAEL*) Burned anything down recently?

MICHAEL. (*standing, frustrated*) AHGHGHGHGHGH!!!!!

SAM. Michael, please. Allen, let's not . . .

PAUL. The mayor's a pyro?

BILLY. That's classic!

PAUL. That's why you're here against your will?

MICHAEL. UGHEHEHEH!!!!!

SAM. Michael, please sit down. Michael has done a great job. Since he's been coming to our meetings, he hasn't had one incident with his issue.

PAUL. So, Manchester's still standing? (*PAUL and BILLY laugh, as do a few others*)

MICHAEL. I'm out of here.

SAM. Michael. Please. You know you can't. You're here for the duration tonight, just like the rest of us.

MICHAEL. Watch me.

SAM. Michael, we have a special guest coming tonight, and you have to be here. It's mandatory.

MICHAEL. What?

MABEL. What kind of special guest?

SAM. That's what I've been wanting to tell you. We need to get through our formal introductions and all, but we can't get completely started until our guest arrives. In fact, I'm surprised he's not here yet.

DAVE TRATTNER and his girlfriend/assistant HOLLY Chapman walk up (through the house/audience).

DAVE. I think this is the location.

HOLLY. You still haven't answered me.

DAVE. Holly, this is neither the time nor the place to discuss this.

HOLLY. Nothing is ever the time or the place with you.

DAVE. Look. I didn't choose this assignment. Judge Edwin Martin personally asked me to take this. It was less of a request and more of a demand. Nevertheless, I'm to be here tonight. I have to talk to these people, who, for some reason are important to him.

Back inside: the conversations go back and forth.

MABEL. Who's coming, Sam?

EUGENE. It had better be Louis. He's not here yet.

SAM. I'm sure Louis has a good reason.

MICHAEL. Who's coming, Sam?

SAM. Judge Martin's asked Dave Trattner to come visit with us a little while tonight.

MICHAEL. (*Searching his memory*) Dave Trattner?

MABEL. That name sounds familiar.

HOLLY. Dave, you can't just invite me here to help you again, like every other assignment, and then . . .

DAVE. I didn't invite you here tonight. If you'll remember, I worked very hard to discourage you from coming with me.

HOLLY. That doesn't work on me.

DAVE. Evidently not. I've tried to be as subtle as I can be and as nice as I can be.

PHYLLIS. Didn't I see someone named Dave Trattner on the news the other night?

EUGENE. One of the talking heads shows?

MICHAEL. Dave Trattner! (*recognition beginning to occur*)

HOLLY. Just because you have a Pulitzer on your shelf doesn't mean you can treat me any way you want!

MICHAEL. From the Post AND the Times? Sam!

EUGENE. He won the Peabody, didn't he?

DAVE. And the Peabody . . .

MICHAEL. And the Pulitzer!

DAVE. . . . but that's not important.

MICHAEL. You're bringing a Pulitzer-prize-winning journalist to this meeting?

DAVE. I've never treated you with anything but respect, but I'm tired.

SAM. I'm not bringing anyone here.

MICHAEL. Why?

DAVE. I lead a busy life.

HOLLY. And I don't?

DAVE. Did I say that?

HOLLY. You implied it.

DAVE. No, you assumed it.

HOLLY. You inferred, left it lurking and unspoken.

DAVE. Don't play word games with me.

HOLLY. True colors, huh?

SAM. He's going to be here as per the request of Judge Martin, too, guys. This is bigger than we think.

DAVE. Look. I have to go in here and see this new kind of therapy or "self-help" that Judge Martin is so tied to. He insisted that I come, and that I come tonight. I have to be here, and I'm probably already late, something I never, never, never am when I'm alone.

HOLLY. What is that supposed to mean?

DAVE. It's called an inference, lurking and unspoken.

HOLLY. You're making this nearly impossible to fix.

DAVE. Holly, it can't be fixed. I don't want it fixed. You're driving me crazy.

MICHAEL. This is driving me crazy. My life is over.

HOLLY. No, I'm not.

SAM. No, it's not.

DAVE. I can't think or get a word in edgewise. It's affecting my work.

MICHAEL. This will be the last straw on the camel's back. It'll ruin my career.

PAUL. Evidently something YOU'VE done is ruining your career.

HOLLY. You know what's ruined your work.

MICHAEL. How dare you. You don't know me.

DAVE. You think you know me so well. But you talk and talk and talk and never *know* me at all.

PAUL. I do know you from the city. I actually live in Manchester. I mean your secret's safe with me, but don't pretend there's not one.

HOLLY. I know you too well. You have everyone fooled: successful, powerful, popular, but some of us know your secrets.

SAM. Again, let's calm down. We're not here to argue.

HOLLY. You, Mr. Dave Trattner, are a slave to alcohol. You are a sot and don't even know it.

DAVE. Holly, this conversation is over. I've tried to be nice.

HOLLY. Nice?

SAM. Mr. Trattner has been assigned here. Everything will be totally anonymous.

MATTHEW. That seems to be the word of the day.

SAM. Well, it is. It's what we're about. When Judge Martin called me and told me what was going to happen, that was my primary concern, but before I could even ask, he assured me that Mr. Trattner was here to write about the process, not the people. Evidently, mixed sessions and open thought are more successful that I realized. The judge is adamant that they continue and that Mr. Trattner see what we're doing.

DAVE. Nice. Too nice. I have a job to do. You, yourself are very good at your job, but we're not good together. I appreciate all the help you've given me, but at this point, I don't need the help anymore. It's taking its toll on me.

HOLLY. It's the alcohol.

DAVE. No, it's you.

HOLLY. Like you don't drink.

DAVE. No, I do. I drink. I drink a *lot*. And since I've met you, I've drunk even more! Good grief, what else do I have to say? I tried my best to give you hints that I was going to handle this alone tonight, that it was an assignment that had a judicial bite to it, that I was tired, that I'm exhausted. You're wearing me out and down.

HOLLY. That's quite a mouthful.

DAVE. You came with me and kept asking and asking and asking, and I'm tired of lying.

SAM. I give you my word, to each and every one of you, that your identities will be safe. I'll lead the discussion in such a way that protects you from that kind of harm. You just have to trust me.

HOLLY. So, you admit you lie to me.

PHYLLIS. That was beautiful, Sam.

ANDY. I trust you.

DAVE. To keep from being painfully honest, yes. To keep from saying how much you irritate me. What do you want me to say?

HOLLY. You're sure being honest now.

ALLEN. Okay, Sam.

DAVE. What else can I be? What else?

PAUL. I thought we were in for Alcoholics Anonymous tonight.

DAVE. Tell me.

HOLLY. Well.

SAM. MICHAEL.

MICHAEL. Yes?

48

HOLLY. I guess I know then.

SAM. Please trust me.

HOLLY. You always have your bottle I guess.

MICHAEL. Okay.

DAVE. I have work to do.

HOLLY. Do it.

DAVE. You can come and sit at the back and I'll drive you home later.

HOLLY. Go ahead. I'll find a taxi or something.

DAVE. You can't just go out and find a way home.

HOLLY. I'm a grown woman, Mr. Trattner. I can take care of myself. Go to your little therapy session. *(She walks off.)*

TROY. Are we going to be honest?

SAM. What?

TROY. Tonight. Are we going to be honest? Like we do at least sometimes. Is he here to see the session the way it's done?

PHYLLIS. That's a good question.

TROY. Or just to interview us about how we relate to all this?

EUGENE. So, we're not going to get our session's worth tonight?

SAM. Just be yourself, guys. Reveal what you want. Keep sacred what you hold sacred.

DAVE. *(Who's been watching HOLLY leave. Composes himself, takes out notes, reads)* Sam Kessler. Okay. *(He knocks on the door.)*

PHYLLIS. Is that him?

TROY. It has to be.

ALLEN. Nobody else knocks.

ANDY. I'll get it, Sam! *(He runs to the door and answers it.)* Hello! Hello!

DAVE. Is this the Martin group session meeting?

ANDY. Absolutely.

DAVE. Dave Trattner. And are you Sam?

ANDY. Heavens, no! Me? Sam? I wish! That's our beloved Sam Kessler right over there.

SAM. (*goes to greet him*) Hello, Mr. Trattner. Welcome! (*Most others stand.*)

DAVE. Call me Dave.

SAM. Sure thing, Dave. I'm Sam Kessler. And you can call me Sam.

DAVE. (*Smiling*) I think I will.

SAM. I have to admit. When I got the call from Judge Martin telling me that you were coming tonight, I was in shock. I mean: you're Dave Trattner.

DAVE. Please. No, don't think that. I'm just here to write a story. That's what I do.

SAM. Well, we're here to help you by being nothing more than ourselves. This is the group.

DAVE. Hello, all.

Most respond: "hello, hi," etc.

DAVE. Please sit. Don't stand on account of me. Like I said: I've been asked to be here tonight. It was a bit of a shock for me, too. I haven't covered anything like this, but I'm happy to be here and look forward to getting to know you and your story—or stories.

MICHAEL. What's that supposed to mean?

DAVE. Pardon.

SAM. Oh, Michael.

MICHAEL. You called me Michael.

SAM. (*Slowly, making a direct and blunt, wide-eyed point to Michael*) I know. Didn't you want me to call you by *another* name tonight??

MICHAEL. Oh, okay. Yeah. That's fine.

DAVE. I'm not here to intrude or cause damage. A journalist is not part of the story or even a catalyst for anything in the story. I'm here to observe and learn and share what I find out.

MABEL. You're a smooth talker. I know why you got the Pulitzer.

EUGENE. And the Peabody.

DAVE. Tonight, it's about you.

SAM. Can I get you something to drink?

DAVE. No, my stomach's a little upset tonight. I'll just go ahead and take a seat and let you all get started.

SAM. Oh, I almost forgot. Ola! Ola!

OLA enters.

SAM. This is my daughter, Ola. She helps me with the sessions, makes sure everyone is comfortable.

DAVE. It's nice to meet you, Ola.

She signs.

SAM. She says it's nice to meet you as well.

DAVE. (*a little surprised*) Oh, okay. Well thank you.

She signs.

SAM. Are you sure we can't get you something to drink?

DAVE. Positive. Thank you.

SAM. Okay, Ola. See you in a bit.

She leaves.

SAM. We're going to go ahead and get started again then. We've already talked about a few things tonight, but for the next few minutes, I just want to go over some basics. These sessions, not just for one issue, are our chance to explore a wide variety of problems and concerns that we deal with daily and hourly. Each one of us fights a demon of some kind that doesn't just attack us, but tries to destroy our every waking second. This is our chance to expose our fears and hopefully douse a few fires burning in our minds. We onboard?

A few respond: "Yes."

SAM. Come on, guys. Are we onboard?

Everyone says," yes" a little more enthusiastically.

SAM. I don't want to share too many sordid details, so I'll be a bit careful. For the sake of your safety, as usual, I won't be using last names.

DAVE. Oh, I'll be changing any name I hear.

SAM. Thank you.

MICHAEL. Thank you.

SAM. I'll give a short preview of the kinds of issues we address with these fine folks each week. Not too much. Just an overview.

DAVE. Sounds great.

SAM. Over here we have Eugene. Eugene is a very intelligent young man, but he has been dealing with severe OCD issues for the past few years.

EUGENE. That's quite accurate.

SAM. Then we have Allen. Allen has an intense craving for cigarettes. He has a hard time dealing with his need, but he's doing a good job fighting it. Next, we have Mabel. Just like Allen, she, too, deals with a need, but in her case, it's a strong need for chocolate. It affects her life in many ways, but again like Allen, she is fighting the good fight.

MABEL. It's hard.

SAM. But you're winning.

MABEL. I hope. I could swim in a pool of milk chocolate the size of Lake Michigan right now.

SAM. But you're not.

MABEL. Right.

DAVE. How long have you been without?

MABEL. That's a good way to put it. Good man. Ten months, one week, and three days since my last stumble.

DAVE. Nice.

SAM. We're proud of her.

DAVE. Good job.

SAM. Next we have Shawn. Shawn is a strong guy, and he hides his problems well.

SHAWN. I think I do.

SAM. But Shawn has a need for human touch. Not just the kind of need we all have.

SHAWN. Not at all. I fight all the time to keep from just putting my hand on people's arms or shoulders. I don't mean anything bad by it. I just really like touch. Handshakes, hugs, anything. I spend most of my time avoiding people's personal space, just to keep from having to deal with touching them. I refuse to make anything awkward.

SAM. Thank you, Shawn.

SHAWN. You're welcome.

SAM. Then there's Matthew.

MATTHEW. Be careful with your wording please.

SAM. Okay.

PAUL. He's a hoarder.

MATTHEW. Stop it!

PAUL. We're about truth here, right? Or is all this a lie?

MATTHEW. I'm not a hoarder. I own my own home. I live my life . . .

PAUL. As a hoarder.

MATTHEW. Stop!!!

SAM. Paul, please. Let me handle things.

PAUL. It's your ballgame, Doc.

SAM. Just Sam. That was Paul. He and his friend, Billy, are new to the group tonight. They, like everybody else here, were assigned to it by Judge Martin himself.

DAVE. And what's your story, Big Man?

PAUL. Big Man. I like that. I got nothing to hide. I live for the rush. Every day holds a new adventure. Jumping, climbing, flying, anything you can imagine, I've done it. And I do it every day. In every way.

DAVE. And all this costs money.

PAUL. Indeed, it does. Indeed, it does.

DAVE. And if you're doing it all, it doesn't leave much time to *earn* the money needed to do it all?

PAUL. You're a smart man, Pulitzer.

DAVE. So the award says.

PAUL. Yeah, I got into a bit of trouble. I had to find money for it all somewhere. That's how the Judge got mixed up in my life I guess.

DAVE. And all of you? Can I assume that all of you, even those who love cigarettes and chocolate, all ended up somewhere, somehow, in a mess of some kind that led to some sort of, how shall I put it, intervention?

SAM. Right on the nose, Dave.

DAVE. I see. And you, Big Guy beside the Big Guy?

BILLY. Me?

DAVE. You'd be the one.

BILLY. Fighting.

DAVE. Fighting?

BILLY. Fighting. Anyone, anywhere, 24/7 if I could. Now if I could.

DAVE. Interesting.

BILLY. Totally.

DAVE. You have quite a roster here.

SAM. We do, yes. Since you've met the Brothers Grimm, we'll move along. This is the artist formerly known as Michael.

MICHAEL. Currently. Remember?

SAM. Yes. I'll refrain from too much information about him, other than to say, he has quite the penchant for fires, lots of fires.

DAVE. You must be the mayor of Manchester.

MICHAEL. What??? Dave!

DAVE. Don't worry, Mr. Mayor. I won't tell a soul I met you, but you have to know that I do keep up with events and situations. That's my job.

MICHAEL. I . . .

DAVE. Seriously. Don't worry. You're just another guy here tonight. No political ties will be mentioned in this article. I give you my word.

MICHAEL. (*Hesitates, hard to say*) Thank you.

SAM. Okay. Moving along. This is Troy. Troy has an obsession over his own body. He doesn't think he's strong enough or powerful enough, so he is obsessed with bodybuilding.

TROY. "Obsessed" is a strong word.

ALLEN. It fits us all.

SAM. We've made, what I thought, was quite a bit of headway. We're convincing Troy, that while it's great to get in better shape, to be worried about it every waking second isn't healthy at all.

DAVE. You look great, Troy. No need to go overboard. You're a brick house. Enjoy it!

TROY. I just need to be stronger. I need it.

DAVE. We all do, man. But in other ways.

TROY. And I had an imaginary friend just commit suicide last week, so I'm needing to be strong in his memory.

DAVE. Well, okay. We all deal with it, man.

SAM. AND, we have Andy, whom you met at the door.

DAVE. Hello, again, Andy.

ANDY. Hello, Mr. Trattner!

DAVE. Dave.

ANDY. Dave.

SAM. Andy, has admitted to being a good guy all his life, but in the past few years, he's become consumed by, how can I put it?

ANDY. I'm no dummy. I can tell you.

SAM. Okay.

ANDY. I'm a people pleaser. 100%. Hard core. I can't stand if the people around me are unhappy or uneasy in any way. I'm constantly, and I mean constantly, thinking of something to do or say that can help someone else or make them feel better about anything they're doing or saying. I know it gets old. I try to fight it. I have scars from biting my tongue tonight. But it's always on my mind, and I'm trying to rid myself of it. SAM.'s been a big help.

SAM. Thank you, and well-said.

MABEL. You just got less irritating.

SAM. And finally, in our little circle tonight is Phyllis.

DAVE. Hi, Phyllis.

PHYLLIS. Hi, Dave.

SAM. Phyllis also deals with an issue that overwhelms us here a lot.

PHYLLIS. Just come out and say it, Sam. It's okay.

SAM. Phyllis struggles with trichotillomania.

DAVE. Wait a second. That sounds familiar.

PHYLLIS. It's familiar to me every second I breath.

DAVE. Hair.

SAM. Yes.

DAVE. Trichotillomania is a condition in which a person constantly pulls the hair out of her body.

PHYLLIS. Yes. But I'm so much better. I haven't done much tonight. I think about it a lot, but I've learned to control my actions.

DAVE. Good for you, Phyllis.

SAM. And we have one more member who hasn't shown up tonight. He never misses, but tonight, he's not here. His name is Louis, and he deals with various kinds of rotating manias. Lots of delusions.

DAVE. Understood.

SAM. That's really just about everybody.

DAVE. Good. So, what exactly do you guys do that's different from a typical group therapy session? I know it's a mixed therapy, which in and of itself is pretty interesting, to be removed *and* close to another person's struggles at the exact same time. Must make for some great conversations.

SAM. It does.

LOUIS. (*Rushing in*) I've been abducted!!!!!!!

SAM. What?

LOUIS. I've been abducted!!!!! I was taken, removed, examined, explored, probed. You name it: they did it?

EUGENE. Ewww.

SHAWN. They?

LOUIS. Yes, they.

ALLEN. Who are "they"?

LOUIS. The big they. Them. THEY!

MABEL. Are those the same people who say everything? You know: they say money is scarce these days. They say blood's thicker than water. They say . . .

MATTHEW. We get it.

LOUIS. It's not the they-they. It's the THEY-THEY.

TROY. I'm confused.

LOUIS. THEY!!

SAM. Calm down, Louis.

LOUIS. I was abducted. I know what happened.

SAM. Nobody's doubting your sincerity.

LOUIS. Sincerity?

MICHAEL. That's what you think happened . . .

LOUIS. Think? Think?

Through the door walks Judge Edwin MARTIN and his son, DARREN. They are dressed nicely. Judge MARTIN is obviously sick. DARREN carries a large briefcase or chest.

MARTIN. Good evening, all.

SAM. Judge Martin?

DAVE. What a surprise.

They all stand.

MARTIN. Please, please, keep your seats. Sit.

All, except SAM. and DAVE, sit.

MARTIN. It's so delightful to see you all here tonight. I'm very pleased with the progress that you all have made within the confines of this group. And I'm glad to see our last two members join the ranks.

SAM. Everyone is here and accounted for.

MARTIN. Yes, I saw Louis Willis finally arrive tonight. How are you, Louis?

LOUIS. Scared out of my mind.

SAM. Louis.

LOUIS. Well, I am. And no one believes me for anything.

MARTIN. Louis, I'm sure anything you say is presented with total honesty and
conviction.

LOUIS. Thank you, Judge.

MARTIN. Oh, forgive my rudeness. I have someone I'd like for you to meet. This is my
son, Darren. He's come with me tonight to see you all.

SAM. Darren.

DAVE AND THE REST. Hello.

DARREN. It's a pleasure to meet you all. I've been looking forward to this night for a
long time.

MARTIN. Let's not get ahead of ourselves.

MABEL. *(to MATTHEW)* What does that mean?

MATTHEW. It means I don't like this.

MARTIN. Everything will make sense soon. This is a night of celebration.

MICHAEL. Celebration.

MARTIN. Yes, I've invited Mr. Trattner here tonight, as you know, to record the
triumphs and joys and successes of this wonderful group.

PAUL. How successful is this group again?

MARTIN. You have no idea.

PAUL. Evidently not.

MARTIN. Darren, would you go ahead and open the case.

DARREN. Yes, sir.

MARTIN. I believe in honoring benchmarks, celebrating small victories, and large
accomplishments. I also believe in ceremony. That's why I'm so glad to have
you all here tonight. Ceremonies are incomplete with members of the family

missing. But tonight, here and now, we're all accounted for.

SAM. I think I'm a little confused, sir.

MARTIN. Please don't be. It's simple. Look. I know several of you suffer with what can only be called addiction, and that monster rears an ugly head, so champagne or a good old-fashioned whiskey would be out of the question. But if you'll allow me a safe, modern variation: nice pure water. If you'll notice, those of you who worry about OCD issues, these are sealed bottles. I have no interest in raising your level of anxiety. Please take one.

DARREN passes out small bottles of water.

MARTIN. I won't waste a lot of your time. I just ask that you indulge me a simple toast to the success of our program and a sincere wish for an end to all of your struggles.

MARTIN takes a special bottle to SAM.

MARTIN. Here, Sam. This one is yours.

SAM. Thank you.

ANDY. This is actually a very nice sentiment.

MARTIN pulls DARREN aside.

MARTIN. Take this drink two doors down. You know what to do.

DARREN. Yes, sir. (*He leaves.*)

MARTIN. Back to our festivities. Oh, I almost forgot. SAM., is your sweet daughter here tonight?

SAM. Yes, she's back in the kitchen I think—reading.

MARTIN. Well, I would love for her to join us in the toast if you don't mind.

SAM. No problem at all. I'll go get her. (*He walks to the kitchen.*)

DAVE. Judge Martin, while we're waiting on Sam and his daughter, I want to thank you for coming tonight. It's nice to see a public official take such an interest in the people he helps.

SAM. reenters with OLA.

SAM. Ola, this is Judge Martin.

MARTIN. It's very nice to meet you, Ola.

OLA signs.

SAM. She responds in like fashion.

MARTIN. Excellent. (*Hands her a bottle. Coughs.*) Sorry for the coughing. I'm not totally well. I spend my life chasing dreams like the rest of you do, often finding they take their toll. (*Beat*) Please, everyone. Bottles up.

Everyone removes caps and lifts bottles.

MARTIN. As I have said and not to belabor a point: I'm proud of your courage and of the progress each one of you is making. May your futures be bright and free from conflict and may any sorrows you have melt away this evening. Cheers.

GROUP. Cheers.

They all drink.

ALLEN. I've never toasted with water before.

TROY. I've never toasted before.

MARTIN. You all did a fine job.

SAM. Thank you for the kind words, Judge Martin.

MARTIN. You know, I, too, find that stress can cause problems in my life. You know how I cope?

EUGENE. How?

MARTIN. Crossword puzzles. The hardest ones I can find. The ones that frustrate me. Then when I have a breakthrough, several words seem to solve themselves at once. And then, every once in a while, all the words line up, almost presenting themselves in time to me.

ANDY. That's dumb.

SAM. Andy!

ANDY. Did I say that?

MARTIN. That's perfectly okay. It may be . . . dumb.

SAM. Andy, you said something unpleasant.

ANDY. I never say unpleasant things. I never say anything rude!

SAM. That's a side of you I've never seen.

PHYLLIS. You might have had some sort of a breakthrough.

ANDY. You think?

MABEL. Let's try something. Go wash my car.

ANDY. Go wash your own car. (*He puts his hand on his mouth in the delight.*) Did you hear that? (*He begins laughing.*)

SHAWN. That's great, dude.

EUGENE. Wait a minute!

SHAWN. I know. I know. I said "dude." I'm not going to change the way I talk just to . . .

EUGENE. No. It's not that. Say it again.

SHAWN. Say what again?

EUGENE. What you told Andy.

SHAWN. "That's great, dude?"

EUGENE makes a small, contained scream.

SAM. What's wrong, Eugene?

EUGENE. It didn't bother me.

ALLEN. What didn't bother you?

EUGENE. Usually, everything that comes out of every one of your mouths irritates me because it's foolish, incoherent, or grammatically incorrect. But Shawn said, "dude." Did you hear that? He said" dude." I just said "dude."

SHAWN. What are you getting at, Eugene?

EUGENE. Dude. Dude. Dude. Dude. It doesn't bother me. It's not making my skin crawl. I'm not irritated with any of you right now!

SAM. Well, Judge Martin, it looks like you came on a very productive night.

MARTIN. That seems to be the case, doesn't it?

ALLEN. Wait a second. There is no part of me that isn't in any way craving a cigarette right now.

PHYLLIS. Oh my gosh! The idea of touching my own hair is repulsive to me.

SHAWN. (*to MATTHEW*) Wait a minute! I don't want to touch any of you. In fact, the idea of it makes me sick.

PAUL. That scared me a little. Why? Did I just say "scared"?

DAVE. Okay. What's going on here?

BILLY. I'm kind of scared, too. I don't like this.

MATTHEW. Okay. I just want to throw away everything I own.

EUGENE. Whoa, dude! (*He starts to giggle.*)

MICHAEL. I can't believe I'm saying this, but I don't think I like . . . fire anymore. I think.

DAVE. What's going on?!

TROY. I hate Arnold Schwarzenegger!!

BILLY. That guy scares me. (*Shocked at his own statement*)

MABEL. Are you telling me I'm about to start disliking chocolate? (*Beat*) Yeah. There it went.

LOUIS. (*Screaming, almost confessing*) There were no aliens! It was just a family of raccoons! Their claws were cold.

DAVE. (*to SAM.*) Is this some sort of a joke? Have you guys played a giant trick on me? If so, I don't have time for this and I don't like it.

DARREN enters.

MARTIN. Everything completed?

DARREN. Yes, sir. Did you complete your toast?

MARTIN. We did indeed.

DARREN. Good.

SAM. I have no clue what's going on here. For years, each of these people has dealt with issues. We've talked about them forever. And now, I don't know what's happened.

MARTIN. Mr. Trattner, you're having a difficult evening. Would you like a good, strong drink?

DAVE. Absolutely not! That sounds completely ... (*shocked*)

MARTIN. Sounds completely what, Mr. Trattner?

DARREN. Disgusting?

DAVE. Yeah. Disgusting. But how can ... ?

SAM. With all due respect, Judge Martin, I'd like to know what's going on.

It has been obvious for the last few minutes and remains obvious that Judge MARTIN is a very sick, very weak man. He has to sit, lean, and constantly gather his balance. He also appears to be dizzy and coughs quite a bit. His son tends to him as much as he can.

MARTIN. I'm both amazed and thrilled to see the results that we've seen tonight. In all of my years of planning and in all of my highest hopes, I never would've dreamed that the results would be so thorough and so exciting.

SAM. Results? We didn't even have a real session tonight.

DARREN. It has nothing to do with the session. It's never had anything to do with the session.

MARTIN. Darren, please. Let me handle this.

DARREN. Yes, sir.

MARTIN. Unless I'm terribly mistaken, I believe that each of you will find that your ailment, your obsession, or your problem has either been greatly reduced or completely eliminated.

EUGENE. But how's that possible? We've done nothing since you've arrived but ...

MATTHEW. Nothing but . . .

SAM. Toast.

ALLEN. The toast.

BILLY. But that was nothing but bottled water.

MARTIN. A little bit more than.

ANDY. What?

EUGENE. You gave us some sort of drug?

MABEL. Without even asking us?

MARTIN. It's a very long story.

PAUL. You drugged us? Yes or no?

MARTIN. Technically, yes, but there's more to it than you realize.

SAM. Judge Martin, you do realize that what you have done is extremely illegal?

MARTIN. I was correcting a problem, Sam.

SAM. Each of these people has had problems, Judge. To correct these problems . . .

MARTIN. (*Interrupting*) I didn't say problems. I said a̲ problem.

DAVE. Mr. Martin, I've always held you in high esteem. But I have to tell you: I'm extremely concerned. This is a major offense.

MARTIN. Mr. Trattner, do you feel better than you did a few minutes ago?

DAVE. That's not the point.

MARTIN. Please answer my question.

DAVE. Yes, I do, but . . .

MARTIN. (*Talking to everyone*) Does each of you feel better than you did a few minutes ago?

Everyone answers in the affirmative. There is a little bit of excitement in the air as people realize that their infirmities are disappearing.

DARREN. Dad, I know you didn't want to, but you're going to have to tell them the whole story.

MARTIN. I suppose it's inevitable.

SAM. Judge Martin, please tell us what's going on.

MARTIN. Before I begin, I'd like to ask each of you to forgive me. I've done questionable things in my life, but in each case, I did what I thought was right in order to save people's lives. I've been planning this night for years. It has taken me many years to get all of you in one place at one time.

MICHAEL. Years? Us? What do you mean? We haven't known each other very long at all.

MARTIN. Again, that may be true technically, but you were all together once before.

MABEL. Once before?

The judge is getting weaker and weaker as he tells his tale.

MARTIN. Mr. Trattner, how long have you been suffering with chronic alcoholism?

DAVE. Well, I've always drank.

MARTIN. *Chronic* alcoholism.

DAVE. Seven or eight years.

MARTIN. Allen, how long have you been smoking four to five packs of cigarettes per day?

ALAN. I don't know. Seven, eight, nine years.

MARTIN. Matthew, when did you begin your collections?

MATTHEW. A little over . . . seven years ago.

PAUL. Wait a minute. That's the same time that I started dealing with my issues.

At once, everyone begins talking to each other, confirming the fact that they themselves have been dealing with their problems for around seven to eight years.

MARTIN. Everyone, everyone, please listen.

SAM. What are you saying? Are you saying this was all triggered at the same time? Are you saying this isn't internal? What are you getting at?

Judge MARTIN begins coughing. His son consoles him and continues the tale himself.

DARREN. My father is a wonderful man. He's lived an amazing life dedicated to helping everyone in his path. He first went to school as a chemistry major and then eventually went prelaw before becoming a lawyer and then a judge. I don't think I've ever seen anyone fairer in my entire life.

MARTIN. Please. This isn't about me.

DARREN. This is completely about you. As you know, when you do the right thing for long enough, someone's going to get very angry. You can't administer justice the way it's supposed to be administered and keep everyone happy. Fifteen years ago, dad had to deal with a very unhappy man, Ted Mitchell. He was a bad seed by every definition. Nearly every crime you could imagine, he had committed. Then when dad put him away, that man stood there staring at Dad and told him that he would pay for having done this to him, and that the people my father loved would suffer. But Dad put him away anyway. About seven years later, Ted Mitchell escaped from prison, and he fulfilled his promise. I was about 12 when this mad man kidnapped me. It's amazing that I'm alive today considering all the things he told me he was going to do to me. He took me, and he left a note telling my parents that if they contacted the police, he would kill me. I guess since dad had dealt with him before, he believed his threats. I don't even think he wanted money. He wanted revenge. And he wanted to make it last as long as he could. So, almost eight years ago, I was taken to Baltimore. And my dad did just about the only thing he knew to do. He hired a detective to try to find us. He caught up with us at a little restaurant called the Sunshine Cafe next door to the Raven City Inn off of 95.

TROY. Oh, I've been there before.

MABEL. Wait a minute. That sounds familiar.

MATTHEW. I was in Baltimore about seven years ago.

BILLY. I lived with my dad there about . . . Oh.

SAM. Baltimore? That was . . .

DAVE. Baltimore?

DARREN. My dad couldn't call the police. I'd be dead today had he done that. He saved my life.

EUGENE. What exactly did he do?

DARREN. Keep in mind that my dad knew this man forward and backward. He'd read all of the psychological records. He knew almost everything there was to know about him. He knew his hopes and his fears and what made him tick and what kept him awake at night. And his Achilles' heel was debilitating fear. He was a sociopath. He had no conscious. He didn't care about anyone but himself. The only way to get him was through his weakness. Any other decision made would've caused him to kill me and several other people, including many of you.

SHAWN. Us?

DARREN. Yes.

MARTIN. You were all there that day.

DARREN. Any misstep, and we would have all died. My dad told the detective to take him out. To take the chemical compound and put it in his water.

ALLEN. The chemical compound?

DARREN. The chemical compound that takes any traits you have, any weakness you have, any possible addiction you have, any psychological disorder you have, and multiplies it numerous times to the point that it can incapacitate you, to make a man swimming in fear collapse upon himself.

PHYLLIS. I think I'm going to be sick.

MARTIN. It has a happy ending.

DARREN. It went into the water pitcher. Mitchell got a large dose. But before anything else could be done, the waitress had diluted the rest of the pitcher with fresh water and began pouring glasses across the restaurant, your glasses. The detective was helpless. The solution had not yet begun to work on Mitchell, and yet she was pouring diluted versions into your glasses. If you remember at all, Mitchell collapsed in the restaurant, could not handle the amount given to him.

MICHAEL. I remember that.

DARREN. It was at that point the detective could come, tend to this "heart attack" victim, and rescue me. All carefully orchestrated, no lives lost.

MABEL. But you ruined our lives. We've had to deal with these illnesses for years.

DARREN. You all went your separate ways as soon as Mitchell collapsed, before Dad even arrived. Right or wrong, the detective's focus was on saving my life. By the time that part had settled, you were all gone.

ANDY. Back home to deal with all this.

DARREN. He's spent every waking minute since that day trying to find you, trying to get you together in one location so that he could provide you the antidote. I've been with him every step of the way, feeling total guilt over the fact that my life was saved while yours were ruined. It's been our goal to put an end to your suffering and to ours.

SHAWN. I don't know if I would've believed you had told me this before we drank.

MARTIN. That's why I gave you the water. Please tell me you feel better.

EUGENE. I don't know if . . .

MARTIN. Do you feel better?

EUGENE. Yes.

BILLY. Yes.

MATTHEW. Yes.

PHYLLIS. Yes.

LOUIS. (*screaming as he runs out of the building*). Yippee!

DARREN. I'll take that as a yes.

SAM. Baltimore. Seven years ago. (*Has a huge epiphany*) Oh my! (*He runs out through the kitchen.*)

OLA looks confused, but she stays to watch--out of curiosity.

DAVE sits with his head in his hands for a long time.

SHAWN. I'm not going to lie. I, for one, am happy. Whatever the case, I feel normal again. I don't appreciate being drugged--twice. But thank you for setting it right. I want to get out of here. Are we done?

DARREN. It seems your counselor has gone. Our story's finished.

SHAWN. I'm out of here. Matthew, need a ride?

MICHAEL. I'm going home. I'll never see any of you again. Never even acknowledge me in public. (*He leaves.*)

SHAWN. MATTHEW, do you need a ride?

MATTHEW. I guess. (*walks up to MARTIN*) Son or no son, I don't appreciate being manipulated. Let's go.

He and SHAWN leave.

TROY. Are we really free to go?

ANDY. Just go already if you want.

DARREN. You're free.

TROY. Well, thanks, I think. Glad you're alive and all.

DARREN. Thank you.

TROY leaves.

PHYLLIS. (*calls after TROY*) Troy, wait. Thank you, Mr. Martin. Both of you. You've given me my life back. Troy! Wait. (*to them*) I have something that I've been needing to do.

She leaves.

DARREN. I guess it's about time I get Dad home. This has been a long time coming, and he's had a very long day.

DARREN starts to organize their things.

EUGENE. Wait.

DARREN. Yes.

EUGENE. I want it back.

BILLY. Yes, me too

DARREN. What do you mean?

EUGENE. I wanted back the way it was an hour ago.

DARREN. Are you serious?

ALLEN. Me, too.

ANDY. Absolutely. It has to go back to the way it was.

DARREN. Back to a world of addiction and suffering?

PAUL. Back to me the way I know myself. I had no desire to come here at all tonight. I had nothing that I wanted to fix. That substance from seven years ago didn't disrupt my system. It fixed my system.

MABEL. I don't like this at all. At least when I had an addiction to chocolate, I craved something. Now I don't care. I don't like not caring.

ALLEN. You poisoned us once seven years ago and now you come in here and try to change who we are. Have you ever stopped to realize that what happened us then is part of who we are now? You just adjusted the clock and robbed us of seven years. But the world still has that seven years on us.

DARREN. You want your problems back?

EUGENE. We want ourselves back. These things you call problems and quirks are part of who we are.

ALLEN. Sure, I want to quit smoking, but I want to do it on my terms, not on yours.

SAM. enters. He is clearly worried and extremely concerned.

SAM. I can't find her. I can't find her anywhere.

MABEL. Who, SAM.?

SAM. Deanne. My wife. She's lived in that bedroom for years, but she's not there.

OLA begins to panic. SAM. notices her.

SAM. It'll be okay, Sweetheart. We'll find her. She's got to be around here somewhere. Let's look in the kitchen and in the other meeting rooms.

SAM. and OLA leave the room in different directions.

ANDY. Did you go to Sam's house?

DARREN notices that his father is not moving.

DARREN. Dad? Dad? (*He shakes his father.*) Dad?

BILLY. Do you have any of the original compound?

DARREN. DAD! Oh, Dad! (*He starts to cry.*)

PAUL. I really think it would be a good idea if you told us how we could get ahold of the original formula.

EUGENE. I don't like this new feeling at all, and I need to go back to the way we were not long ago.

DARREN is openly weeping at the corpse of his father.

ANDY. I want this fixed now.

PAUL. Right now.

MABEL. We would appreciate an answer.

DAVE. (*Standing up*) I demand that you restore me. You've stolen my career. You've stolen my soul. I want it back.

SAM. and OLA enter from different doors simultaneously.

SAM. Any luck?

OLA signs and shakes her head.

At that moment, the front door enters and a clearly happy and disheveled DEANNA Kessler enters. All other conversations stop.

DEANNA. (*free from pain*) Sam! Ola! Sweetheart!!!

OLA's and SAM.'s mouths fly open in disbelief.

OLA. Momma!!!!!!!!!!!!

Sam grabs his chest and drops from a heart attack.

Lights out---FAST!

Lowery Christopher Collins (Chris) has been an educator and writer for over thirty years. He is currently a professor of English at Panola College in Carthage, Texas. He has taught at the high school, middle school, and elementary school levels and as an English and literature instructor at the college and university level. For several years, he was a high school theatre director and a gifted education consultant. He's been honored with several teaching awards, including the Young Audiences of Northeast Texas Outstanding Service to the Profession Award and the Kennedy Center's Steven Sondheim Award for being one of the most "Inspirational Teachers" in the U.S.

He is also an award-winning playwright of over thirty scripts, a weekly newspaper columnist, a short story writer, a poet, a pianist, a vocalist, a songwriter, a recording artist with Daywind Studios, the founder and artistic director of Stagelands Theatre Company, an aspiring novelist, and a (former) choir director. He's taught a variety of classes, from rhetoric and composition to literature to acting to the Bible.

He holds a Bachelor of Arts Degree in English and History and a Master of Arts Degree in English from Stephen F. Austin State University in Texas and has served on fine arts and gifted education committees as well as on a board of governors for a small playhouse.

In addition to his interests in teaching, directing, and writing, he has a fondness for lighthouses, windmills, filmmaking, salsa, sculpture, Flannery O'Connor, travel, dominos, guacamole, social media, genetics, Maine, landscaping, pillows, gospel music, Shakespeare, marbles, YouTube, quantum physics, movies, weird jokes, maps, trees, cold rooms, and Texas.

He can be reached at mrchriscollins@hotmail.com,

on Facebook at www.facebook.com/tofferdreams,

on Twitter at "tofferdreams,"

and at his website: www.ChristopherCollinsOnline.com.

To view Christopher Collins's books and other writing, visit Ponderlake Publishing, at www.ponderlake.com.